Gymnastics
JITTERS

text by Margaret Gurevich

illustrations by Katie Wood

raintree

a Capstone company — publishers for children

Raintree is an imprint of Capstone Global Library Limited, a company incorporated in England and Wales having its registered office at 264 Banbury Road, Oxford, OX2 7DY – Registered company number: 6695582

www.raintree.co.uk
myorders@raintree.co.uk

Graphic Designer: Heather Kindseth
Production Specialist: Michelle Biedscheid
Illustrated by Katie Wood
Originated by Capstone Global Library Ltd
Printed and bound in China

ISBN 978 1 4747 3227 7
20 19 18 17 16
10 9 8 7 6 5 4 3 2 1

British Library Cataloguing in Publication Data
A full catalogue record for this book is available from the British Library.

CONTENTS

Chapter one

A GOLD MEDAL

The judge lifted his card, and the music began. Dana raised her fingers in the air and pulsed her hips to the beat. Then she ran.

Her toes bounced off the mat, and she hurled herself through the air. She did a flip before landing back on the mat. The crowd applauded, and Dana finished with three back handsprings.

"Nice work, Dana!" her team cheered.

She smiled to herself. She knew she nailed the routine. Only a cartwheel and split left. Not a wobble on either move.

"You did it! You did it!" cheered her best friend and co-captain Mallory.

"Atta girl," said Miss Jasmine.

Dana beamed as she sat back in the stands and waited for the other girls to complete their routines. She was happy with her routine.

"Wish me luck, girl," said Mallory. She unzipped her River City Raiders jacket and went to warm up on the uneven bars.

"You don't need it," said Dana, smiling. She was superstitious about wishing other gymnasts luck. And saying "break a leg" would be disastrous.

Mallory jogged to the bars shaking her head. Dana could swear she was grinning.

Dana rubbed her palms together and blew on them. The Halsey Gym wasn't cold, but she shivered. She watched her teammates Connie and Paula on the beam and vault. Their routines were flawless.

Then it was Mallory's turn. Dana sucked in her breath and felt an arm around her. Miss Jasmine always knew when to calm her nerves.

"Mal will do great," she said. "I bet you're more nervous than she is."

Dana nodded and tried to smile. Mallory grabbed the lower bar and raised her body into a handstand. Dana counted the hold count in her head. She knew Mallory wanted to hold it for two full seconds.

Mallory swung her legs down and raised her legs straight over her head again. She did three rotations on the high bar before landing with a firm grip on the lower bar and turning again.

Dana held her breath as Mallory prepared for her dismount. Since they spent most of their waking hours together, each member of the team knew the others' routines.

Dana and the other girls leaned in and grabbed hands as Mallory flung herself to the top bar again. She rotated four times, flew through the air and completed a somersault.

The stadium applauded as Mallory planted her feet on the mat, then raised herself to full height. Her smile was huge.

"She did it!" screamed Dana. She didn't have to look at the scoreboard to know that Mallory earned a high score.

Miss Jasmine gathered her team in a big hug as soon as Mallory reached the stands.

"This is big, ladies," said their coach as she pointed to the board. There were the results of their hard work.

A gold medal for the River City Raiders.

Chapter two

THE NEXT STEP

A week later, the team couldn't pass their school's trophy case without stopping and smiling at their trophy. Miss Jasmine smiled too as she saw her team admiring their prize.

"There may be another trophy up there soon," Miss Jasmine said. "Your huge win has moved the Raiders to the next leg of the competition. This is a first in River City history."

Dana and her team looked at each other, their faces questioning. They knew they'd done better than anyone expected this year. They knew winning a gold medal was huge. But they were too busy enjoying that success to think about what came next.

Then Dana looked at Paula's panicked face. What came next was clear.

"The next level is against the Sumner Superiors, isn't it?" asked Paula.

"That's right," said Miss Jasmine.

The Sumner Superiors were the best gymnastics team at their level. They were also the meanest. They didn't just fight with skills. They fought with words and dirty looks. Their goal was to psych out the other teams.

Dana remembered hearing that Shelly, the Superiors' captain, once put itching powder in another team's leotards.

"I know the Superiors have a bad reputation," Dana said.

Paula smirked. "That's being nice," she said. "The kids in detention have a reputation. Put them in a room with the Superiors? My money is on Sumner."

Dana put her fears out of her head. As a team captain, she had to put on a brave front.

"Fine," she said. "But who says we can't beat them?"

Connie bounced up and down. Her blond braid bounced behind her. Dana smiled. She loved that Connie could always tell when the captains needed backup.

"That's right," said Connie. "We have the skill and the muscle." She flexed her arms and everyone laughed.

Connie continued, "Besides, you can't get far by playing dirty. I think they just have a bad reputation because they always win and people are jealous."

Dana chimed in, "Makes sense. If we keep winning, people may start saying things about us."

Miss Jasmine smiled. "Nice pep talk," she said. "Keep it coming."

Soon Dana's fear was replaced with hope. Who said the Raiders couldn't win this one?

Chapter three

INTIMIDATION

On Saturday morning, the Raiders were at the Halsey Gymnasium early for their scheduled workout. They stretched and watched the Superiors finish their practice.

"There's no way we're going to win this," moaned Connie.

"Think positive," said Dana. She stood on her tiptoes to stretch her calves. Her eyes did not leave Shelly, who was on the other side of the gym doing her floor routine.

"She's right, Connie," said Paula. "How's this? I'm *positive* we're not going to win." She laughed.

"Very funny!" said Dana. "Now, no more of that negative talk. I know we can do this."

The music stopped in the gym, and the Superiors packed up their gear. The Superiors' coach brought them into a huddle for a secret talk and blew his whistle. The girls picked up their duffle bags. He blew the whistle again. The team got into a straight line. A third whistle and they marched single file to the exit.

"That's what we call intimidation," Miss Jasmine whispered to Dana.

"Well, it's working," Dana whispered back. "They even leave the gym perfectly!"

"Okay, team," said Miss Jasmine. When no one moved, she spoke louder. "Girls, if we're going to win, we cannot just stand around. I can train all of you to follow commands, too. It means nothing. Now let's practise!"

Dana and her team slowly walked into the now empty gym. All of their energy was gone. Each girl was lost in thought and more than a little nervous.

"I want to see strength out there!" Miss Jasmine said. "I want to see power! You can do it!"

Of course we can, thought Dana. *Mallory rocks the uneven bars. I own the floor. Connie's a whiz at beam, and Paula is fantastic on vault. If the Superiors want to beat us, they'll have to work at it.*

Dana continued giving herself a pep talk as she walked to the mat. Her teammates had obviously done the same thing. They were completely focused. Suddenly, she stumbled as she was shoved from behind.

"So sorry," came Shelly's familiar nasal voice. "I could have sworn I left my ribbons in here."

Dana looked around the gym. She was not surprised there were no ribbons.

Shelly laughed and looked in her duffel bag. "Oh my goodness!" she said. "They're right here. Silly me."

"Funny how you didn't think to look there first," said Dana, finding her voice. "I mean, that's what a normal person would do."

Shelly scowled. She said, "When you focus on the floor routine as much as I do, there's little room in your brain to think about anything else. See you around." She smirked and ran out of the gym.

Dana's blood boiled. *I'll show her who's focused,* she thought. She ran to the mat and turned on her music.

Dana ran as fast as she could and launched into three back handsprings. She focused on every movement in her routine. Shelly couldn't be further from her mind.

Chapter four

A NEW PLAN

As the Raiders sat in their favourite
lunchspot, Veggie Haven, the morning's
bad vibes vanished.

"This place has the best veggie burgers
ever. You can actually taste the celery!" said
Connie. She took a large bite of her bun.

Paula made a face.

"Don't knock it until you've tried it, Miss
Spinach Lasagna," said Connie.

The other girls laughed and dug into their veggie dishes. Even Dana, who was a meatball fanatic, loved the Haven. She twirled her courgette spaghetti around her fork. Then she lifted it high in the air and swooped it into her mouth.

"Perfection," she said. She thought a minute. "That should be our new name! The River City Perfections."

"That would be cool," said Paula. "However, I think we're stuck with the River City Raiders."

Dana sighed. "I know," she said. "Superiors just sounds so annoying. I want a name that says how good we are, too."

"Do we have to ruin a perfectly awesome lunch by talking about the Superiors?" Connie asked.

Dana pushed her plate away. "They always make me lose my appetite," she said.

Paula rolled her eyes and kept eating. "Are you going to finish your garlic bread, Dana?" she asked with her mouth full.

Dana shook her head. Paula eagerly grabbed it. "Gotta keep up my strength if we're going to beat the Superiors," she said.

"Here's what I'm thinking," said Mallory. She licked tomato sauce off her finger. "All we need to do is practise and focus. I know the Superiors are good, but so are we. We're going to keep our head in the game, ignore them and do our best."

"Speaking of the Superiors," mumbled Dana, nodding towards the door. A group of girls in Superiors jackets entered Veggie Haven.

"I think it's time to go," Dana said. "We have work to do."

"I don't want them to think we're running away from them," said Connie.

"If we run anywhere," said Dana, "it will be to the gym. From now on, whenever they enter that gym, I want them to know we've been there."

"How?" asked Connie. "By leaving Mallory's smelly trainers under the trampoline?"

"Not a bad idea," said Dana with a laugh, "but that's not what I had in mind. Don't worry. I have a plan."

Chapter five

THE PLAN TAKES SHAPE

When the girls got to the gym, it was empty. There were no signs that the Superiors had been there.

Dana took in a deep breath. "Just pure sweat," she said. "No Sumner stink at all."

Mallory laughed and said, "Like you can really tell when they've been here."

"I can," said Paula. "The air feels cold and evil after they've practised."

"It's not evil you smell after their practice," said Mallory. "It's the awful perfume they wear." She pretended to gag.

Connie's eyes lit up. "That's it!" she said. "I always wondered why I stunk like daffodils after I left this gym."

Dana did a middle split and leaned forwards, elbows touching the ground. "Who wears perfume to work out?"

Connie stretched her thighs and hamstrings. "People who want us to know they were here," she guessed.

Paula bounced on the springboard and somersaulted in the air over the vault. She wobbled on the landing and made a face. "I thought we were going to play by new rules, Dana," she said. "Don't you have ideas?"

Dana ran to the mat and did two back handsprings. She stumbled a little on her landing. "Not until we've given this practice our all," she said. "I don't know about you, but I can use all the focus I can get."

The girls split up to work on their own equipment. Dana turned on her music and practised back handsprings until all her landings and releases were perfect. Then she walked over to the uneven bars to watch Mallory.

As much as Dana worried about whether she would succeed, she never worried about Mallory. Mallory always appeared to be in control. This calmed Dana.

Dana stood far enough from the bars not to distract her friend, but close enough to see all of Mallory's tiniest moves.

Dana watched as Mallory mounted the bar. Her shoulders were open like they should be, and her legs looked straight. Dana knew the handstand was next. She held her breath until Mallory finished her count.

Dana knew that the release was next. But she wasn't worried. Mallory released and flipped twice in the air. Mallory stuck the landing and raised her hands high in a V.

Dana clapped. "That was amazing, Mallory," she said.

Mallory blushed. "My legs were a little bent," she said.

"Just barely," Dana said.

"It's still a deduction," said Mallory. "We can't afford that."

Dana wanted to tell her not to worry, but Mallory was right. "You'll get it," Dana said. "You always do."

Mallory smiled, and she and Dana walked to meet the rest of the team. They looked sweaty but satisfied.

"Nice work today," said Dana to the team.

"Thanks," said Paula. "Do we get to have fun now?"

Dana slapped her hand to her forehead. In all her concentration, she had forgotten about her little plan. "I almost forgot," she said. She grabbed her bag and gave all the Raiders scissors, construction paper and marker pens. Then she explained her plan.

"I feel like I'm in play school again," said Mallory, giggling.

Connie followed Dana's lead and cut out an R. Then she drew pink polka dots on it. "Perfection," she said, smiling.

Paula cut out her R and frowned. "You don't think we'll get in trouble for this?" she said.

"We're not doing anything bad," said Dana grinning. "Just marking our territory."

"All done," said Mallory.

Dana gathered the other girls' Rs and slipped them places around the gym: one beside the balance beam, another under the mat used for floor exercise, and others at the foot of the vault and uneven bars.

"I think the Superiors will like the new decorations," said Paula with a laugh.

Chapter six

PLAY FAIR

Miss Jasmine did not like the new gym decorations.

"Girls," she said at practice. "I was at the gym this morning. I saw some interesting artwork. Anyone care to fill me in?"

No one did. They stared at their school's gym floor.

"Maybe someone else decided to leave random letter *R*s around the gym?"

Dana frowned. "But Miss Jasmine," she said, "we didn't mess up equipment. We didn't even put them in anyone's way."

Paula piped in, "I even checked all the handbooks when I got home. No rules about leaving letters around."

Miss Jasmine sighed. "It's not against the rules," she admitted. "You won't get in trouble from the Gymnastics Association or anything like that. But I don't like it. We don't need to do that."

"We just wanted to let the Superiors know they can't scare us," mumbled Mallory.

Miss Jasmine's voice softened. "I know that, Mal," she said. "I understand it has not been easy for you girls to ignore the Superiors. My gosh, their stinky perfume is enough to make me want to leave!"

The girls laughed.

"I just don't want you to stoop to their level," Miss Jasmine said. "I know it seems harmless, but we must play fair."

"Got it," said Mallory. Dana sulked.

"Good," said Miss Jasmine. "From now on, I want you thinking about how you can beat them with hard work, not mind games."

Chapter seven

THE SHOWDOWN

Two days later, the Raiders entered the gym ready to work hard. The Superiors were already there and hogging the equipment. On weekdays, the rule was that teams rotated on the equipment. But it was obvious to Dana that the Superiors followed their own rules.

"They're hanging all over the uneven bars," Mallory complained. "They're not even practising."

Dana frowned. Miss Jasmine expected the Raiders to play fair. Why didn't the Superiors' coach expect the same?

"Come on," said Dana. She took Mallory's hand and walked to the uneven bars.

"You done hanging out?" Dana said as the Superiors lounged on the bars.

Tori glanced at her teammates. "You guys done?" she asked them as she stretched out.

"Nope," said Shelly. She glared at Mallory and Dana. Dana remembered the way Shelly had smirked when she came back for her ribbons.

Dana thought about the right thing to do. She stayed calm and asked, "Will you be practising long?"

A Sumner girl named Tori pointed her nail-polished finger at Dana, saying, "We'll stay here as long as we want. Since when did you start calling the shots?"

Dana's temper rose. "When did *you*?" she asked.

Something twinkled behind Shelly's eyes. Dana wondered if Shelly was surprised that Dana was standing up for her team. *I know I'm surprised*, Dana thought.

"Look," began Tori, stepping in front of the other girls.

Dana felt a tug on her arm, and Mallory stepped in.

"No. You look," Mallory said. "If you win, it will only be because you're not letting the rest of us practise. That doesn't show you're better."

Dana saw tears in Mallory's eyes and hoped the Superiors would leave before they noticed.

Tori opened her mouth to yell, but Shelly cut her off. "Forget it," said Shelly. "They are not worth our time."

With that, the Sumner group moved on to the trampoline. Dana was still fuming and tried to calm herself. Focus. They don't matter.

Dana saw Mallory's eyes clear up. She put her hand on her shoulder. "You okay?" she asked her friend. "Thanks for jumping in like that."

Mallory nodded. "I saw you were trying to play by the rules, and thought you could use some help," she said.

Dana headed over to the mat. This time it took a few minutes for the music to draw her in. Once it did, it was just her and the floor. She saw her routine in her mind and followed it. The splits, forward rolls and flips soon became easy

"Nice work," said Paula when Dana paused to catch her breath. Dana jumped. She didn't know anyone was watching.

"Thanks," said Dana.

"I'm not just talking about the floor," said Paula. "You were great with the Superiors, too. I don't think I would have said anything."

Dana shrugged and said, "I thought about what Miss Jasmine said. I just wanted to practise and win the right way."

Paula patted her on the back. "Whatever you're doing, keep it up," she said.

Dana blushed. "Thanks," she said. Then she noticed the quiet of the gym. She looked around. All the teams were practising together and sharing all the equipment. Even the Superiors.

Chapter eight

A BAD PRACTICE

The next day, Dana walked into the gym and breathed in deeply. It was one week before the championships, but the Halsey Gymnasium was empty. She liked practising with her team, but there was something special having the entire space all to herself.

She stretched and then plugged in the CD player by the wall. She put in her floor routine CD and started moving.

First the hip shake, then the toe point. Then Dana geared up for her front handsprings. She ran and did three in a row, her legs reaching high into the air. The next part was her favourite. She planted the soles of her feet on the mat and did two flips – one forwards, the other backwards.

Dana landed perfectly, but her heel fell outside the boundary line of the mat. This rarely happened to her anymore, and it made her nervous. It was so easy to lose the championship from that kind of deduction.

She started her routine again and focused on the flips. Again, her heel went out of bounds. Sweat formed on her upper lip. *This can't be happening*, she thought.

She tried again. This time she started the flips well in front of the boundaries. It didn't help.

Dana panicked. It wasn't fun being in the gym anymore. Shaking, she packed up her things.

On her way out, she spotted Mallory. The last thing Dana wanted to do was stay in the gym, but she knew Mallory liked the support.

"You okay?" Mallory asked Dana. "You look freaked out."

Dana's voice shook. She said, "I'm having some trouble with my routine."

"It happens," Mallory said. "You'll get it. Isn't that what you always tell me?"

Dana smiled. She hoped watching Mallory would calm her down like it usually did.

Mallory dipped her hands into the chalk bucket beside the uneven bars.

"The chalk feels different," she said to Dana. "Huh. Weird."

Dana watched Mallory shake her head, something she did when she was trying to focus. Then she grabbed the lower bar.

Mallory's fingers slipped and Dana panicked. She saw Mallory's fingers tighten on the bar. She lifted herself up with her forearms. She stuck her toes out in front of her and held the pose for a second. Then she jumped to the higher bar. She swung around and around, but something wasn't right.

Was it Dana's imagination, or was the bar higher than usual? Mallory lowered herself and almost fell. Dana gasped. She had never seen Mallory struggle with that move before.

Dana watched Mallory restart her routine. Dana held her breath as Mallory worked through her routine. Her body whipped through the air easily. Then came the dismount.

Instead of two flips, Mallory only had enough height to do one rotation. She fell over as soon as she landed on the mat. Dana stared at her friend, stunned. The last time Mallory had fallen over on a dismount was years ago.

"Mallory!" yelled Paula and Connie, bursting through the gym. "What just happened?"

"I – I don't know," Mallory stammered.

"I've been having problems, too," said Dana quietly.

"Probably nerves," said Paula.

"Probably," said Dana. She hoped that was all it was.

She and Mallory stayed to watch Connie and Paula. Hopefully their practices would go better.

Dana watched Connie hop onto the beam. She pointed her toes as she walked. She did a small jump. No wobbles. Flip time. Dana breathed a sigh of relief as Connie somersaulted and stuck the landing on the beam. It was time for the dismount. Dana covered her eyes and peeked through the slits between her fingers. Connie cartwheeled off the beam and cheered when she landed flawlessly on the mat.

"Awesome!" yelled Dana.

Paula clapped behind her. "Nice work!" she shouted.

Now it was Paula's turn. Dana, Connie and Mallory turned to watch. Paula always made the vault look easy. She ran and jumped on the springboard before launching herself over the vault.

In all the time the Raiders had known Paula, she had never once messed up this move. Not even at practice!

Paula ran and pushed off the vault, but she couldn't stick the landing. Dana could tell Paula was embarrassed.

Dana tried to hide her worry. "Shake it off. It happens," she said, echoing Mallory's earlier words.

Paula slid down to the floor and sat down. "Not to me," she said.

And then everyone started to talk at once. The panic was out of control.

"Girls!" Miss Jasmine yelled, trying to be heard over the Raiders' panicked voices. "Please tell me what the problem is."

Dana swallowed. She willed herself not to cry. "We're off our game," she said. "We can't hit our jumps or landings. I've never seen anything like this before."

"I'm sure it's just pre-competition jitters. Happens to everyone," Miss Jasmine replied.

"But not to us," said Mallory. "We've been in competitions before and never stumbled like this."

"It's the Superiors!" said Paula. "They must have put a curse on the gym or something."

Miss Jasmine laughed. "That's just silly," she said. "Forget about the Superiors. Do your best, and you can't go wrong."

Paula jumped up. "You weren't there!" she insisted. "Mallory said the chalk felt funny. Dana kept going out of bounds on her floor routine. I fell on the vault!"

Dana saw something change in Miss Jasmine's eyes while Paula talked. "Take the day off today," Miss Jasmine said.

"But–!" Mallory said.

"There's no time!" Connie said.

"We have to focus!" Paula added.

"Enough," said Miss Jasmine. Her voice was quiet but stern. "Veg in front of the television, go to the mall, do some homework. I don't want you in the Halsey Gym today. Understood?"

The girls pouted but nodded.

"I'll see you tomorrow," said Miss Jasmine.

* * *

The next day, the Halsey Gymnasium was extra busy. There was just one more day until the championship. After a day off, Miss Jasmine had allowed the Raiders to practise again. Dana was glad. She wanted to practise.

Dana did back handsprings on the mat for her floor routine. This time she landed within bounds. Paula cleared the vault and landed with her feet centimetres apart. She didn't even hop on the landing.

The chalk felt right on Mallory's hands. She cleared the lower bar as she did three rotations on the higher bar. She released her grip and glided through the air. She stuck her landing, too. Connie walked the beam with poise, her arms spread out.

"Bravo, ladies, bravo," said Miss Jasmine, clapping. "I think that is the best practice I've seen yet."

"And the Superiors have been absent all day. Coincidence? I think not," said Paula, smiling.

"I know it sounds weird," said Connie, "but I think she's right."

Miss Jasmine's voice was stern. "No more talk like that," she said. "It just fills your head with worry. Only think about yourselves. You will succeed."

Chapter nine

THE CHAMPIONSHIP

The Raiders filled their thoughts with success. Dana hoped Miss Jasmine was right.

The day of the championship, Dana was extra nervous. She hopped from foot to foot, full of energy. When she couldn't stand waiting, she did handsprings and cartwheels to release her restlessness. She grinned when her heels landed within bounds every time.

There were two minutes to go before the meet started, and Dana didn't see the Superiors anywhere.

It bugged Dana that the Superiors thought they didn't need the extra gym time. *Just think about yourself,* she reminded herself. *You can't control anyone else.*

Dana glanced at the line-up. Paula was first. She caught Paula's eye and gave her a thumbs-up. She was glad Paula was first. Paula liked going first, because then she didn't have to worry the rest of the competition.

Dana saw the judges stand. The room grew silent as the national anthem played. Then the starting bell rang. The head judge nodded at Paula, and she ran down the runway.

Paula jumped on the springboard and placed her palms on the vaulting table to help propel her through the air.

Before Dana could exhale, Paula's feet were planted firmly on the mat. She raised her arms high in the air for the finish. Dana cheered.

Shortly after Paula was done, Dana performed her floor routine. She didn't step out of bounds or have any problems. After her routine, Dana ran to get a drink. She wasn't paying much attention and bumped into someone.

"I'm sorry," Dana said. Then she looked up. Her jaw dropped when she saw a tearful Shelly.

"Are you all right?" asked Dana. "Why aren't you in the gym?"

"We can't compete today," said Shelly.

"Why?" Dana asked, confused.

Shelly sighed. "We were disqualified," she said.

Dana's eyes grew wide. She asked, "Why?"

Shelly sniffled. "Tori and another girl messed with all the equipment," she said. "I had no idea! It was so stupid. If I knew, I would have stopped them. Who wants to win that way?"

Dana nodded. She remembered Miss Jasmine's very similar words. "Have you been here the whole time?" Dana asked.

"Yes," Shelly said. Just watching you guys. You guys are doing great. I so wanted to compete today. It's not fair." Tears ran down her cheeks.

"I'm sorry," Dana said. "I really am."

"Me, too," said Shelly. "You were really good on the floor. I bet you guys win."

"Thanks," said Dana.

Shelly shrugged. "Just telling it like it is," she said. "Don't think we're friends or anything now. I plan on beating you fair and square next year." She winked.

Dana smiled. She knew she could handle the competition. "I'm looking forwards to it," she said.

She sprinted back into the gym as the judges called first place for the team awards.

The Raiders squealed and ran to stand at the top of the three-stepped platform. They were beyond excited!

Miss Jasmine gave them a thumbs-up. Dana realised that her coach must have sensed something was wrong the day she didn't want them in the gym.

Mallory poked Dana in the side. She pointed to the gym's entrance where Shelly stood.

"Why didn't Shelly and the Superiors compete today?" Mallory whispered.

"It's a long story," said Dana. "But let's just say playing fair and working hard is the way to go."

"You don't have to tell me twice," said Mallory. She smiled and held the first place medal around her neck tightly. Dana did the same.

About the author

Margaret Gurevich has wanted to be a writer since second grade. She has written for many magazines and currently writes young adult and secondary school books. She lives with her husband, son and two furry kitties.

About the illustrator

Katie Wood fell in love with drawing when she was very small. Since graduating from Loughborough University School of Art and Design in 2004, she has been living her dream working as a freelance illustrator. From her studio in Leicester, England, she creates bright and lively illustrations for books and magazines all over the world.

GLOSSARY

CARTWHEEL sideways handspring with arms and legs straight out

DEDUCTION amount that is taken away from the score

DISMOUNT move used to get off a piece of gymnastics equipment

DISQUALIFIED prevented from taking part in the action

HANDSPRING flip forwards or backwards where the feet go over the head and then land back on the ground

REPUTATION your worth or character judged by other people

ROUTINE a set of moves a gymnast performs

SPRINGBOARD flexible board that helps a gymnast jump high into the air

SURPASSED to be better than another thing

COMPREHENSION QUESTIONS

1. If you had to pick one gymnastics event to perform, what would it be and why?

2. Dana is the captain of the gymnastics team. What kind of qualities does a captain need to have? Does Dana have those qualities?

3. Do you think it was a good idea for Miss Jasmine to give the girls a day off before the big meet? Why or why not? Why did Miss Jasmine do that?

WRITING PROMPTS

1. With Dana's guidance, the Raiders find an interesting way to get revenge and intimidate the Superiors. Write a paragraph describing what you would have done if you were the Raiders.

2. The Superiors and the Raiders are rivals. Is it good to have a rival? Write a list of reasons to defend your answer.

3. In the end, the Superiors were disqualified. Write a new ending to the story, but this time, they didn't get disqualified. In your rewrite, be sure to include who wins.

The word "gymnastics" comes from a Greek word meaning "to exercise".

Gymnastics was one of the nine sports included in the first modern-day Olympic Games in 1896.

Men's gymnastics was first entered into the Olympic games in 1896. Women first competed in Olympic gymnastics competitions in the 1920s.

The most decorated gymnast is Russian Larissa Latynina. She has 18 Olympic medals!

Most gymnasts retire in their late teens or early 20s. This may seem young, but most major gymnasts begin their careers at the age of 2 or 3.

In 2006, the scoring system for gymnastics was completely changed. In the new system, there are two separate scores: one for difficulty and one for execution.

In the early 1800s, vaulting horses looked like real horses. They even had heads and tails! In 2001, the vaulting horse was replaced with the vaulting table.